"Come on, BLOOM . . .

. . . it's mushy

and
slushy
and
delicious
in here!"

BLOG

A LITTLE BOOK ABOUT

FINDING LOVE

BLOOM!

Written and Illustrated by MARIA VAN LIESHOUT

Designed by MOLLY LEACH

FEIWEL AND FRIENDS   NEW YORK

"No thanks,"
said BLOOM.

"I'm not in the mood for puddles."

She felt like
DANCING
and
SINGING . . .

. . . and stretching out under

the flowers.

BLOOM closed her eyes and
took in a deep, sweet breath.

"I LOVE flowers," she sighed.

A flutter brushed by.

"A flying flower!
A FLYING,
DANCING
flower!" BLOOM gasped.

"He is the most BEAUTIFUL thing I've ever seen!"

"Come and get me,
FLYING FLOWER,

so I can dance

in the sky with you."

The FLYING FLOWER drifted down.

They looked into
each other's eyes
for a long time.

"I love you," whispered BLOOM.

But the FLYING FLOWER
t w i r l e d   a w a y.

Higher and
higher.

"Hey, come back!
Don't leave me down here!"

BLOOM's eyes followed
the FLYING FLOWER

until he was a dancing dot in the sky.

"FLYING
FLOWE

R!"

BLOOM plopped down

and let out a long sigh.

"He loves me,
he loves me not,
he loves me,
he . . .

Oh, forget this!"

She closed her eyes and sniffed.
She felt alone.

"BLOOM, will you please come
play in the puddle with me?"

BLOOM shook her head.

"I can't. My heart is broken," she whispered.

"I will never love again," BLOOM sobbed.

"BLOOM . . . ?

. . . I have something for you."

BLOOM blushed.

"For ME?"

"Are you in the mood for THIS puddle, BLOOM?"

BLOOM blinked and took in a deep, sweet breath.

"I LOVE IT,"
she sighed.

FOR PETER

A Feiwel and Friends Book
An Imprint of Holtzbrinck Publishers

Library of Congress Cataloging-in-Publication Data Available

ISBN-13: 978-0-312-36913-2
ISBN-10: 0-312-36913-1

First Edition: January 2008

10 9 8 7 6 5 4 3 2 1

www.feiwelandfriends.com